Ladder to the Moon

MAYA SOETORO-NG

illustrated by
YUYI MORALES

CANDLEWICK PRESS

First edition 2011

Library of Congress Cataloging-in-Publication Data is available.

Library of Congress Catalog Card Number 2010039183

ISBN 978-0-7636-4570-0

11 12 13 14 15 16 SCP 10 9 8 7 6 5 4 3 2 1

Printed in Humen, Dongguan, China

This book was typeset in Cygnet.
The illustrations were created with acrylics on paper and then digitally manipulated.

Candlewick Press
99 Dover Street
Somerville, Massachusetts 02144

visit us at www.candlewick.com

This book is dedicated to
my mother and my daughters.
May we all continue to grow and learn.

M. S.-N.

To my sisters, Elizabeth and Magaly,
and my brother, Mario Alejandro—
together we are stronger than we imagined.

Y. M.

One cool new evening,
Suhaila asked her mama,
"What was Grandma Annie like?"
"She was like the moon," her mother replied.
"Full, soft, and curious.
Your grandma would wrap her arms
around the whole world if she could."
Mama gave Suhaila a hug.
"You have Grandma Annie's hands,"
she said.

Later, Suhaila lay in her pajamas,
the moonlight coming through her open window.
She looked at her hands, frontside and back,
and wondered what else she had gotten from her grandma.

As the night deepened and the crickets grew loud,
Suhaila wondered and waited.
It seemed like something was about to happen.
Then, as though in answer to her wondering,
a golden ladder appeared at the edge of the sill.

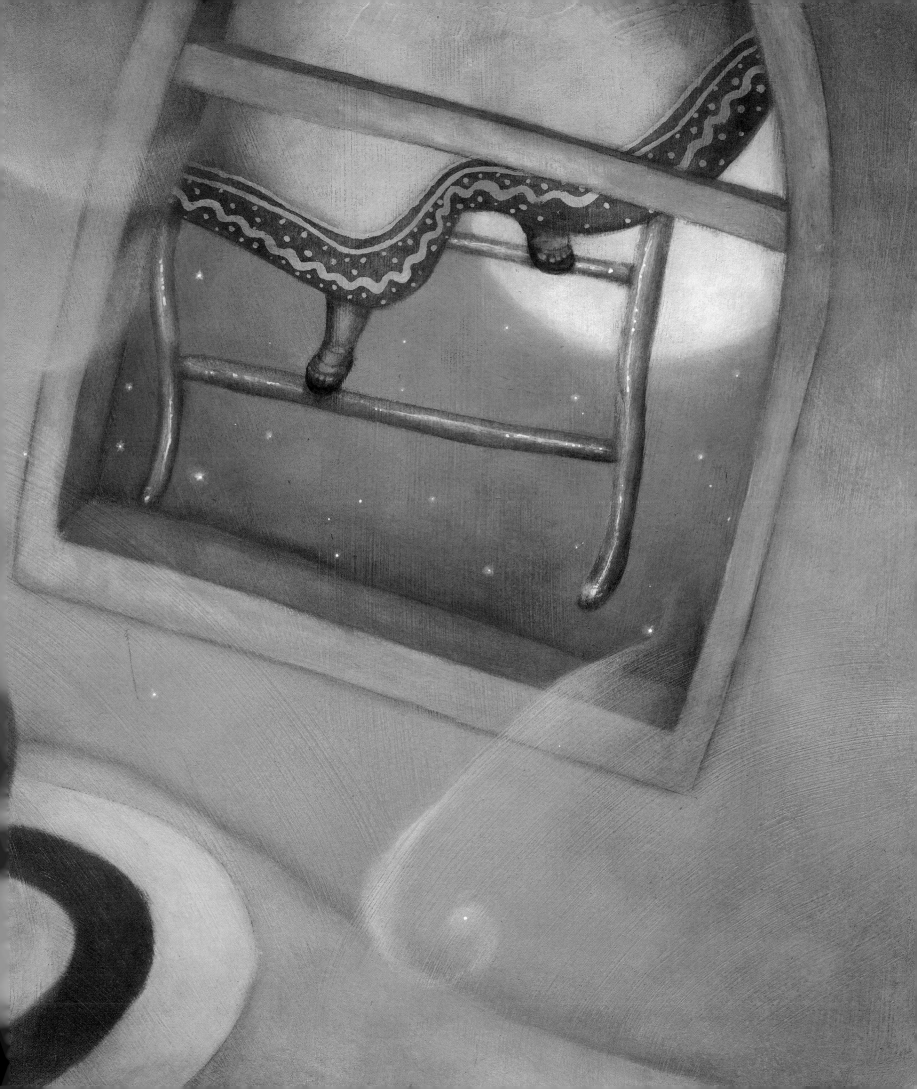

There, right on the lowest rung,
stood Suhaila's grandmother,
her silver-bangled arms outstretched and tinkling.
"Do you want an adventure, my dimpled child?"
Suhaila nodded twice, the second time more certainly.
Then she tossed herself out of bed like a tumbleweed
and ran to the window.

Together, step-by-step, they climbed that ladder
in the path carved by the moon's glow.

From the top rung, Grandma Annie jumped to the moon first.

She let herself grow wider and wider,

wider than the biggest crater.

Then Suhaila jumped, too, into Grandma Annie's soft, waiting lap.

Grandma Annie wrapped her arms around Suhaila's chest,

taking the shiver out of the child.

The two looked back toward Earth,
and Suhaila tried to be brave about feeling so far from home.
"What fun!" said Annie.
"What now?" asked Suhaila.
"Listen," said Annie. "Listen."

The moon is a gray place, it's true, but
the songs of the moon are plenty.
Some are plain and some fancy,
but Suhaila listened to them all, and through listening,
she knew more than she had known before.
With each new song, she smiled and felt stronger,
until the edges of her smile nudged her Grandma Annie
and they too knew each other completely.
Sometimes a smile is strong enough to do that.

"I hear other voices," Grandma Annie said then.
Together they gazed down at the earth below.

A fifty-foot wave was sweeping
from the ocean to the land,
and through swirling waters,
swimmers struggled up toward the surface.
"Kick hard!" Annie encouraged them. "Swim!"
Tilting her head toward her granddaughter, she asked,
"Shall we invite them to join us, little one?"
"May we? We have lots of room," Suhaila responded.

Annie nodded and let her voice drift down.

"Come dance and get warm, babies," Annie urged.

And when the next giant wave crested,

all the children leaped high like flying fish.

Suhaila and Annie caught them by their fingertips

and pulled them up to the moon.

Draping scarves around their shoulders,

they swung the children round and round

until they could all laugh again, loud and long.

Then Grandma Annie paused and whispered,

"I taste other troubles."

Suhaila tasted the air, too, and through tasting,

she knew more than she had known before.

On the ground below,
two sisters climbed down
two tall towers that trembled
and swayed on quaking soil.
"Hang on tight," Annie urged.
When the earth stopped shaking,
Annie and Suhaila watched the sisters
wipe dust from their faces
and stick out their tongues
to catch some soft rain.

"Come bathe and drink with us," Annie invited them.

"Will they know what to do, Grandma?" Suhaila asked.

"Do they know how to get here?"

"Don't worry, honey," Annie reassured her.

"They're stronger than they realize."

Sure enough, Suhaila watched the sisters
weave a shimmering spiral and begin to climb.
Grandma Annie embraced the young women at the landing.
Together they scrubbed themselves clean in falls of mist
and drank sweet moondew from silver teacups.

When the sisters were refreshed, they spoke to Annie and Suhaila.
"There is still so much to do. There are fires to be tended,
gardens to be weeded, and kapok trees to be seeded."
"We'll work together," Annie promised.
"We'll throw in our hearts and minds,
and work with our hands to make the land a little more kind."
And for sure they would: together they'd build
bridges and buildings and bonds between people.

Looking back at Earth, Grandma Annie spoke again.
"I feel faith moving the air down there," she said.
"They're praying."
"For what?" asked Suhaila.
"For one another, and for us," Annie told her.
"And to make the fighting stop."

Setting down her teacup, Suhaila stood, and felt it then,
and, through feeling, knew more than she had known before.

Looking past the golden ladder, she spotted people whose hands pointed
upward from a synagogue, a temple, a mosque, and a steepled church.
One by one, every person was finding his or her own path to the moon,
each path connecting with the others in hope's massive stream.

The moon crew was getting large now.
Everyone sat and traded stories—
stories about courage in canyons and discoveries in the desert.
Stories about people who had lost their languages
and stories about the poor and powerless.
"All these people who need us are people just like you and me,
do you see?" asked Annie after the last tale was told.

Suhaila washed her eyes and did see and, through seeing,
knew more than she had known before.

When Suhaila and Grandma Annie
looked down again, they saw a baby boy
being born from the center of a stalk of corn.
A frail great-grandmother left her cliffside home,
straightened her stooped spine,
and became strong again, just long enough
to help the baby take his very first step.

Then Grandma Annie watched as Suhaila, all by herself,
reached out and took the great-grandmother's hand,
helping her onto the ladder.
Together they climbed,
one of them old and one still quite new.

All the boys and girls on the moon,
all the men and women,
were now part of the moon's hum.
Their silhouettes could be seen from far below
and gave a feeling of plenty to those who had little.
Their dancing movements gave feelings of freedom
to those who were trapped in small spaces.
Those who had been fighting stopped
when they heard the moon's song
and saw its light filling nooks and streams.

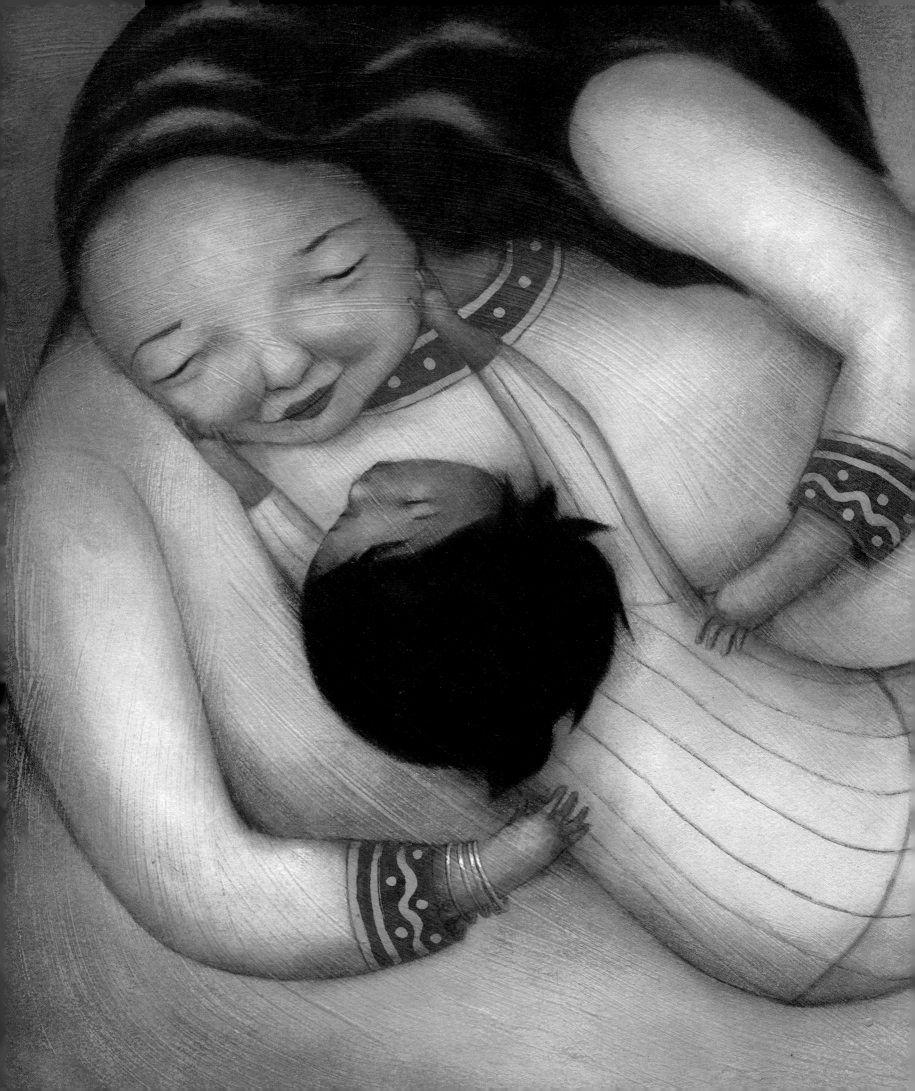

Eventually, Suhaila turned to her grandmother and again nodded twice.

Grandma Annie's nose twitched and her lip trembled with love.

"I suppose it's time for you to go back?"

"Yes," said Suhaila. "Mama misses me, I'm sure. Will you be OK?"

"Oh, yes, little pumpkin," Annie replied.

"I'm so happy that we had this time."

With a snuggle and a smooch they parted.
Looking back just once, Suhaila
slid down moonbeams straight into her bed.
She sat for a quiet half moment, feeling proud
for having helped others heal—
for having helped others learn to move forward
and upward and around.

Together, those of us left on Earth
would plant seeds in soft soil.
Grandma Annie would send tides to nourish them
and weave a net of love around us all.

"Mama, I'm home,"
Suhaila called out into the hallway.
"Mama, I met her!"

"I'm in here, baby.
Come.
Tell me everything."

Author's Note

When I was nine, living in Semarang on the island of Java, my mother gave me a postcard of the 1958 Georgia O'Keeffe painting *Ladder to the Moon.* I loved it. A sturdy yet delicate ladder hung suspended over the silhouetted desert, and above it, slightly to the left, was a soft half-moon. The moon wasn't the focus, I remember; the ladder wasn't even actually pointing to it. It was a pretty thing in the distance. The real focus of the painting was the ladder. The journey was what mattered—life's wondrous journey of discovery.

My mother was a remarkable woman. She would get down on the floor and really play with my brother and me. She built us a kiln for making pottery, and she made toys with us to remind us to relish our childhood freedom. But above all, my mother was a storyteller. She loved listening to stories and reading them to us. She would share the stories of faraway people while sitting in a hammock and looking up toward the clouds. She would create stories about nearby people while sitting around a table surrounded by friends. These stories about heroic journeys and love of every kind are a large part of what made me decide to become a teacher and have become the very foundation of what I teach. When I was a teenager, Mom would wake me up at night to gaze at the moon. Though I failed to fully appreciate the beauty of those midnight moon-gazings then, now I hunger to have them back.

My daughter Suhaila was born a full decade after my mother died of ovarian and uterine cancer. Becoming a parent made me think of my own mother with both intense grief and profound gratitude. More than anything, I wished that my mother and my daughter could have known and loved each other. I hoped that I could teach Suhaila some of the many things I learned as I grew up witnessing my mother's extraordinary compassion and empathy. It was then that I decided to unite grandmother and grandchild through a story in which my mother could meet one of her granddaughters and share the moon with her. They could become part of the moon's light, and as Suhaila climbed the ladder, she would climb toward a more expansive vista and learn the meaning of service. She would watch her grandmother heal and shelter those who had suffered through natural and man-made tragedies, and eventually become the one to reach down, help up, and heal.

This book is dedicated to my mother and my daughters. Though they are separated by breath and years, we honor the strength and the moon that they will always share.

—Maya Soetoro-Ng

Illustrator's Note

I knew I was meant to create art for this book from the moment I first read the manuscript. However, while I felt a deep connection to the story, I also had many questions. What does faith look like? How can inner strength be represented in an image? Would children understand my interpretation of growth toward a higher self? I am a great believer in personal mythology and the strength and learning found in the stories of our sisters and brothers, our parents and grandparents, our ancestors, and ourselves. And so, in my desire to best illustrate *Ladder to the Moon*, I decided to depict in my work some stories of struggle and growth, pain and healing, and death and life that I have heard through the years.

So you will find the image of a caring dog like the one the Aztecs believed to be a person's companion in life and later again on the journey of death. The illustration of people telling stories by the fire is seeded with lines from traditional narratives, as well as from stories that friends have told me of events that happened to their families.

I imagined every character in this book to have a voice and a story that needed to be heard—stories of creation, such as the legend that tells of humanity being created from the corn; real-life stories of women and their children fighting for life and dignity; stories of men using their tribe's wisdom to take care of their community; and ultimately the story of Suhaila and Annie, a grandchild and her grandmother, reaching toward each other to learn, to love, and to grow together in their service to others.

What an honor to have added my voice to this story.

—Yuyi Morales